P9-CSH-221

The Snoop

The Snoop

JANE RESH THOMAS
Illustrated by Ronald Himler

Clarion Books
New York

Clarion Books
a Houghton Mifflin Company imprint
215 Park Avenue South, New York, NY 10003
Text copyright © 1999 by Jane Resh Thomas.
Illustrations copyright © 1999 by Ronald Himler.
The text is 14/18-pt. Classic Garamond.
The illustrations for this book were executed in pencil and black oil paint
with turpentine wash on frosted acetate.
Book design by Carol Goldenberg.
Printed in the USA.

Library of Congress Cataloging-in-Publication Data

Thomas, Jane Resh.
The snoop / Jane Resh Thomas ; illustrated by Ronald Himler.
p.   cm.
Summary: Although her grandmother admonishes her not to snoop while
they visit friends on a farm, Ellen cannot control her curiosity, which often
gets her into trouble.
ISBN 0-395-85821-6
[1. Curiosity—Fiction. 2. Grandmothers—Fiction. 3. Behavior—Fiction.]
I. Himler, Ronald, ill. II. Title.
PZ7.T36695Sn   1999
[Fic]—dc21   98-37955
CIP   AC

KPT 10 9 8 7 6 5 4 3 2 1

*To my students, who have taught me
most of what I know*

—J.R.T.

Contents

The Snoop

ONE

No Animals

"WHERE ARE THE other animals?" Ellen scratched a collie dog's ears. But the barn doors were closed, the pens were empty, and the chicken coop was locked up tight. "Are your cows and horses in the barn?"

"No animals but me and Janet here," said L.J., pointing to his wife and rubbing the slight stubble of white whiskers that made his jaw look frosted.

Ellen looked out across the cornfields that stretched in all directions from the house on the hill. Then she looked at Bon, her grandmother. No animals?

Before this weekend visit with her old friends, Bon had described Janet's and L.J.'s farm. Hearing about the barn and the cornfields and the creek, Ellen had imagined how she would feed the goats and sheep and little soft-nosed calves that would nuzzle her hand. Ducks and geese would fly up from her feet when she crossed the farmyard. If she had known that there weren't any animals, she never would have left home for this first trip away from Mom and Dad. What was a farm without animals?

"And Queenie," said Janet, ruffling the dog's fur. "She's an animal. Don't forget Queenie."

"Said 'animals.' Queenie's family," said L.J. He turned to Ellen. "Sold the cows and machines when we rented out the fields. Buy our milk at the grocery. Cheaper than feeding a cow. Easier than shoveling manure, too."

Janet picked up the shopping bag of clothes that Mom had packed for Ellen. She took Bon's hand. "I'll show you where you'll sleep."

Bon followed Janet into the house and up the stairs. L.J. followed Bon, carrying her old worn suitcase. Ellen followed L.J., and Queenie was the end of the parade.

"There's the bathroom." Janet patted the dark hair neatly pinned in a bun at the back of her head, as if the very sight of the bathroom mirror made her think of dressing up. "Over here across the hall is our bedroom. And down here at the end is yours. Right where you always stay, Maryann." That was the name that other people called Bon. Her family always used the name Ellen had made up as a baby, when she couldn't say "Grandma."

"Thank you," Bon said. "But don't fuss, Janet."

Queenie sat down on Ellen's foot.

L.J. put Bon's suitcase on the big high bed. "Lunch about ready?" he asked his wife.

"As soon as our guests have unpacked and cleaned up," said Janet. "I've cleared out the bottom dresser drawer for you, Maryann."

"There's grilled cheese sandwiches," said L.J.

"And tomato soup," said Janet. "When you're ready." And Bon's friends went downstairs.

The room smelled like things that have been stored a long time. Bon changed out of her cotton traveling dress and put on the extra dress she had brought, her good silky one with sprigs

of purple flowers printed on a lavender ground. She brushed her gray hair, even though not a strand was out of place. Bon's hair always stayed where she put it; Ellen thought it wouldn't dare do otherwise.

On one side of the dressing table, Bon laid out her powder and hairbrush and her beautiful silver mirror with the mermaid handle. She put her silky peach undies in the bottom drawer of the big bureau.

"There," she said. "The rest of the drawer is yours. What are you waiting for?"

"I thought there would be cows and horses," Ellen said. "And chickens. And a haystack to slide down. And pigs."

"L.J. can't manage the heavy farm work anymore," said Bon. "But you'll find plenty to do."

"No horses."

"Lunch is ready. Put your clothes away," said Bon, heading down the hall. "And remember what I said on the bus. Act like a lady." She looked at Ellen over the rims of her glasses. "And no snooping."

No Snooping

ELLEN PUT HER blue sweater and T-shirts and
cotton underwear in the bureau drawer. Her
book topped off the pile of belongings. She laid
her toothbrush on the other side of the dressing
table, across from Bon's things. Then she stuffed
her yo-yo in one pocket of her jeans and her
little bag of marbles in the other. Dad had said
that she might need something simple to do in a
place where the TV was rarely turned on.

Sitting down on the puffy upholstered bench,
Ellen flipped the drawer pulls a couple of times.
They were heavy brass, set against a fancy design
carved in different colors of wood. She picked

up Bon's mermaid mirror and looked at her own blue eyes. As usual, her hair stuck out in every direction.

Ellen remembered her overnight visit at Bon's house, the time she had checked the dressing-table drawers to see whether anything had changed. While Bon fried minute steaks and potatoes for supper, Ellen had found the mermaid mirror and looked at herself in the glass. She had stroked the mermaid's scales and long flowing hair with her thumb; the lady seemed to beckon her.

Ellen remembered the next awful moment as clearly as if it were happening now, in Janet's front bedroom. Somehow, like a fish leaping from water, the mirror had flipped out of her hand, turned a cartwheel, and smashed on Bon's shiny wood floor.

Ellen's stomach had flipped, too. She had picked up the mermaid and looked at the empty circle where the glass had been. She had scraped the shattered pieces together with her hand, not caring if they cut her. Reflected in one piece of mirror, she had seen her own blue eye. In another, her grandmother's apron had moved behind Ellen's shoulder.

"Oh, Ellen! You've broken my favorite thing!" Bon had said. "Your grandfather gave it to me before he died in the war." Bon turned Ellen's face toward her. "You know it isn't ladylike to snoop through other people's things."

Although Dad had paid the jewelry store to replace the glass in the precious mirror, Bon had never let Ellen forget. "Curiosity killed the cat," she liked to say.

Now Ellen set the mermaid down and fingered the pull on the wide center drawer in Janet's dressing table. Just looking wouldn't really be snooping. A drawer like that might contain anything. Lace and velvet things. Lipstick. Jewels, even. And she would only look at them.

As Queenie watched with her tail wagging, Ellen slid the drawer open. Little wooden partitions divided the front. Ellen examined the contents of each compartment. Nothing but hair nets in the first one. Then hairpins, big ones, gray.

The third compartment held a string and

many loose beads. Ellen couldn't really see them
unless she touched them. She picked them out
with her fingers and held them in her palm,
turning them over and over. Bright glass beads
they were, each different, each like a tiny, many-
colored eyeball.

"E-l-len!"

Bon's voice startled Ellen. She jumped and accidentally threw the beads into the air. Most of them landed on the rug, but one hit the mirror, and two or three struck the hardwood floor with a noise like firecrackers. They bounced and rolled under furniture.

The clatter made Queenie jump, too. She bumped her nose on the leg of the dressing table.

"Yes!" Ellen rubbed Queenie's nose. The beads would have awakened the cows, if there had been any cows. Even Bon might have heard the noise.

"Lunch is ready. What are you doing up there?"

"My marbles fell," Ellen said. "I'm coming." She wasn't really. In fact, she was scrambling to pick up the scattered beads. With Queenie sniffing at her hand, she gathered them one by one, put them back in their compartment, and closed the drawer as silently as she had opened it. One thing had led to another. Now she had not only snooped—she had lied to Bon.

THREE

Walking the Dog

AFTER THE GRILLED CHEESE sandwiches and tomato soup, Ellen took her yo-yo from her pocket. She put it into L.J.'s outstretched hand.

He inspected the yo-yo's polished wood through the bottom part of his glasses. He rubbed it with his thumb. "Had one just like it when I was a boy." He handed it back. "Let's see your stuff; what can you do with it?"

"Walk-the-Dog," said Ellen. She expertly flipped the yo-yo out of her palm and made it skitter along the floor on the end of its string. Queenie tried to bite it, but Ellen brought the yo-yo up the string and back to her hand.

"I offered to teach her to crochet or tat," said Bon, "but she'd rather mess with that yo-yo."

"When we were girls," said Janet in a reminding tone of voice, "you were always knee-deep in the pond catching minnows. You weren't much for crocheting and tatting then." She set her coffee cup carefully in its saucer.

"Pretty good." L.J. held out his hand again, and Ellen put the yo-yo in it. "Around-the-World," he said. He snapped the yo-yo. It hummed at the end of the string as he swung it above his head, behind his back, and into his hand again.

"Careful of the lights!" said Janet.

"Not bad," said Ellen, taking the yo-yo back. "Rock-a-bye-Baby." She formed a little triangle with the string and swung the spinning yo-yo back and forth through the shape.

"You win," said L.J., holding Ellen's fist up in the air. "Miss Ellen, Champeen Yo-Yo Thrower of the World. Come on outdoors. Show you my garden. No animals, but I'm not entirely retired."

At the side of the house was the biggest garden Ellen had ever seen. A row of zinnias in every

color bordered the plot. Another row of giant
marigolds grew as high as Ellen's hip.

L.J. pointed at a row of short leaves ribbed
with dark red. "Beets," he said. Another row of
tangled leaves grew taller. "Bush beans," said
L.J. Another row was all feathery green.
"Carrots."

He stopped beside a line of a dozen big red
tomato plants that grew inside wire frames.

"Want one?" He placed a huge sun-warmed tomato in Ellen's hand.

"I don't have a knife. How do you eat it?"

"Just like a peach or an apple. Wash the dust off over there at the pump. Go ahead and look around. I've got to catch these tomato worms."

As L.J. picked the big green worms off the plants and collected them in a coffee can, Ellen wandered around the house to the back. She ate the tomato, minding only a little that the juice dripped down her chin. The beads in the dressing table kept coming to her mind. She didn't like the knot in her stomach that snooping and lying had caused, but curiosity drew her anyway. What pretty things might be in the other drawers?

Janet and Bon sat in wicker chairs on the back porch, cutting up beans and peeling peaches for supper. Nobody but Queenie noticed when Ellen went inside and up the stairs.

Four

Around the World

ELLEN WENT STRAIGHT to the bedroom she was sharing with Bon. The sneaking made her heart pound, but only Queenie would know if Ellen checked the other drawers in the dressing table. Besides, nobody but visitors stayed in that bedroom. In a guest room, things didn't belong to any certain person.

Ellen opened the deep drawer under Bon's hairbrush and removed the silk scarves she found there. Nothing but scarves, except for some funny old curlers made of tan leather. She put everything back the same as she had found it.

In the other deep drawer was a box of bath powder. It smelled like lilacs. A small black leather book said *Addresses* on the front in gold letters. The edges of the cover were worn. Ellen opened it to the names of Carmela and Domenico somebody—the spelling was complicated. At the bottom of the address, Ellen could read the word *Italy*.

She flipped through the book. One person lived in Germany, one in Wales, and two in Paris, France. Ellen saw that most of the other addresses were near home. She put the book away under the lilac powder.

Queenie was sitting by the bureau, wagging her tail, inviting Ellen to go ahead and look there, too. Ellen already knew what was in the bottom drawer—her T-shirts and book and Bon's silky peach underwear. Next were blankets sprinkled with mothballs. So that was where the funny smell came from. The next drawer held sweaters with mothballs. In the top were wool pants. And mothballs. The fumes made Ellen's eyes sting.

"Ellen. *E-l-len!*" Bon's voice floated in through the open window. "Where did that girl get to?"

Ellen and Queenie hurried down the stairs, out the side door, and around the house to the porch where Janet and Bon still sat. "Here I am. Just exploring." Now Ellen had lied and snooped and sneaked around besides. Why couldn't she act like a lady, as Bon had told her to do?

Peter Rabbit

LATE IN THE afternoon, Ellen sat in the long shadow of the oak tree in the yard, stroking Queenie's ears. The dog lifted her nose and sniffed the wind. Then she trotted across the yard toward the sweet-corn patch, her nose high, as if she were tracking a trail in the air.

Ellen followed Queenie across the brightly sunlit grass to the edge of the corn. She pushed between two plants, across a row, across another, until she stopped in the middle of the patch. There in the darkness under the corn, Queenie stopped to nose something in the soil.

Ellen knelt beside the dog, waiting for her

eyes to adjust to the deep shadows. The corn
towered over her, each rough leaf rubbing
against others, scratching and rattling like paper.
She could see no farther than a few feet down
the row, and between the corn tassels overhead
to the sky beyond. The place was like a private

little room in the midst of greenness, with a high blue ceiling and a cool brown floor.

Ellen pushed Queenie aside. There at her knees lay what had drawn the dog to this place, a tiny brown rabbit, his white belly soft and motionless under her hand. He looked just like

Peter Rabbit after he lost his slippers and little blue coat. Ellen picked the rabbit up and put his fur to her cheek. He smelled like milk. She closed his hazy eyes.

With Queenie prancing between her feet, Ellen went between two long rows of cornstalks to the end of the patch and knelt again in the brightness there. She blew on the rabbit's silky fur. It lifted and parted to the gray fuzz next to the skin.

"Ellen! Where are you?"

Darn! Ellen had a tight collar around her neck, and Bon held the leash. Her grandmother couldn't let a person out of her sight without calling. Ellen should hide in the corn patch to teach Bon a lesson. She should explore the bridge down the road and play in the creek that she could see meandering across the fields.

But she didn't. Carrying the rabbit between her two hands like treasure, Ellen went toward the porch where Bon and Janet still sat in their rocking chairs. The rabbit's legs hung limp.

"Look," Ellen called. "Look what I found. A baby rabbit."

"A rabbit?" Janet leaned forward in her chair, trying to see across the yard.

"A dead rabbit." Bon leaned away. "Put the nasty thing in the garbage before it draws flies to the house."

"Oh, for goodness sake, Maryann. You're so squeamish these days, anyone would think you'd never had a snake collection," Janet said. "Let the girl show us what she found."

Ellen carefully laid the rabbit on the porch

railing and knelt beside him, examining every part. "He has tiny red veins in his ears," she said. "They look as if an artist drew them with a fine point right on the skin."

She showed Janet. "So they do."

"He's so perfect. Why do you suppose he died?"

"Maybe he was sick," said Janet.

"Maybe it wandered away from its mother. Maybe it was poking around where it didn't belong." Bon kept her hands folded firmly in her lap.

"I want to take him home," said Ellen.

"Yes, you want to keep it—but you can't," said Bon. "It will spoil by tomorrow. Put it back where you found it or in the garbage can."

Ellen went around to the back of the house, where the garbage can stood. She took off the rattly cover. If she put the rabbit back where she had found him, animals would eat him. But he didn't belong in the garbage can, either. No. Whatever Bon thought, Ellen would take the rabbit home and give him a real funeral under the lilac bush, beside her old cat Fluffy.

She went quietly through the back door and up the stairs to the room she shared with Bon. She wrapped the baby rabbit in her sweater and hid him under the bed. She would put him in the bottom of her shopping bag, under her clothes, before she went home. Bon would never know.

That evening in bed, after the lights were out and the house was quiet, Ellen lay beside Bon in a pool of moonlight, listening to the wind in the cornstalks across the yard. An odd smell hung in the air.

Bon raised up on one elbow and sniffed, just like Queenie. "Ellen, what did you do with that rabbit?"

Ellen said nothing.

Bon sat up. "Don't make me hunt it out with my nose, Ellen. Where is it?"

"Under the bed." Even Ellen's tiny voice made the room sound hollow.

Bon turned on the light and went around the end of the bed. She got down on her hands and knees. "You'll have to wash this sweater before you wear it again," she told Ellen. She dropped it on the floor as if it had fleas.

Bon padded downstairs. Ellen heard the back door squeak. The garbage can rattled when the lid went up and again when the lid went down.

Ellen took her sweater under the covers and embraced it, shutting her eyes to hold in her tears. They soaked the pillow anyway.

SIX

Just Looking Around

NEXT MORNING, Ellen stood on the porch with L.J., looking out across the fields. Fog filled the hollows and valleys. The misty air was like damp flannel on Ellen's face. She imagined Peter Rabbit when he was still alive, hopping through the mist at the edge of the garden, where now Queenie nosed the grass.

"It looks like the country of the ghosts," said Ellen.

"Yup. Eerie, all right." L.J. limped across the porch. "Fog makes my joints stiff. Want to play crazy eights until the sun comes out?"

Ellen and L.J. sat at the kitchen table, playing

cards, until Ellen was tired of crazy eights. Then she practiced her yo-yo tricks while the others played bridge and talked about people she didn't know.

She thought about the beads and the address book with the gold letters and the faraway people. What might be in the other closets and drawers upstairs? A daughter had grown up in this house. Ellen had seen her photograph on the television set. Maybe there were dolls. Maybe lace and more jewelry. Maybe letters from Italy and Wales.

Ellen closed the stairway door behind her and crept upstairs as quietly as she could, with Queenie padding behind her. She stood in the hall, listening to the murmurs below. She shouldn't. No snooping, Bon had told her. But yesterday L.J. had invited her to look around. Just looking wouldn't hurt anything, and she had permission anyway.

Ellen tiptoed into the room where Janet and L.J. slept. She would start with the small drawers of the dresser; the letters and jewelry might be there. Queenie sat watching, wagging her tail as Ellen eased one drawer open. She found neatly folded handkerchiefs, some with lace, and a shiny silver necklace.

The floor creaked under her feet. She froze, listening for a change in the voices below. The murmuring continued. But when Ellen moved, the floor creaked again. Chair legs scraped on the linoleum floor in the kitchen. The stairway door opened.

"Ellen?" It was Janet.

But the dresser drawer was stuck. And Ellen couldn't escape without Janet's seeing her. She

stood in the doorway and tried to throw her voice across the hall to the bathroom, the way ventriloquists did. "Yes?"

"What are you doing, dear?" Janet was coming up the stairs. Queenie rushed to meet her.

Ellen's heart pounded in her throat. She pulled the neck of her T-shirt up around her nose, preparing for the shame and the scolding. Janet would scold her and tell Bon. Bon would scold her and tell Mom. Mom would scold her and tell everybody else. Nothing would save Ellen now.

And here stood Janet in the bedroom door, her eyes flicking from Ellen to the open dresser drawer behind her. "Well, is that pesky drawer stuck again?"

"I was only looking around," said Ellen, in a voice so quiet she could hardly hear it herself.

"I wish you had told me you were curious," said Janet. "There isn't much to see, but I'll show you what there is."

Janet showed Ellen the face cream and powder and the small gold earrings in the stuck

drawer and then jiggled it shut. She opened the next drawer down. "Just my underwear, Ellen. Not much to see."

Ellen felt her face get hot with shame.

Janet opened the bottom drawer. "L.J. wears long underwear to keep his stiff knees warm." Queenie was so curious she nearly climbed into the drawer. Janet pushed her back gently and closed it.

Wasn't Janet even angry? Wasn't she going to scold? Maybe she would leave that up to Bon. "*Please* don't tell Bon I was snooping," said Ellen.

"I wouldn't think of telling her anything of the kind," said Janet. She took something out of her pocket. "I found this in the hall. Would you like to know more about it?"

Ellen looked at the glass bead in Janet's hand and nodded.

"L.J. sent me this necklace from Italy, the place where your grandpa was killed. They were both in the army there during World War II." She handed the bead to Ellen. "You can put this one with the others."

Janet waited at the top of the stairs while Ellen did that. "Now I'm going to make an apple pie for supper," said Janet when Ellen returned. "Want to help?"

Ellen hugged Janet. "I'm good at peeling apples," she said.

Janet hugged her back. "I'll bet you are."

Janet put her arm out. Ellen linked her own arm through it. And the two friends headed for the kitchen.

SEVEN

Paying Respect

BON AND L.J. were putting away the cards when Janet and Ellen came into the kitchen.

Bon eyed Ellen. "What's going on?"

"Just a little woman-to-woman conversation," said Janet. She took a bowl of apples out of the cupboard and began to wash them.

Ellen looked out the window toward the corn patch. The glass reflected her own face and Bon's, behind her. Bon was like a hawk studying a frog. Her eyes could pierce iron. She would keep at Ellen until she either lied or confessed.

"Here, you two," said Janet, offering a couple of paring knives. "If the three of us work together, we can peel these apples in no time flat."

Bon wasn't listening. "What were you doing upstairs, Ellen? Did you forget what I told you on the bus?"

Ellen stood up taller, turned, and faced her grandmother. "I'm not a lady, Bon. I was snooping. And my baby rabbit isn't garbage. I'm going to bury him."

"Oh, Ellen! You were snooping when I told you not to?" Bon scowled her most hawkish scowl.

"I wouldn't call it snooping, Maryann," said Janet. "Ellen likes pretty things. And she's adventurous, just like her grandmother. Remember the time our teacher caught you looking through her desk?"

Bon's jaw moved, but no sound came out, as if she wanted to speak but couldn't. At last, she huffed so furiously that Ellen half expected her to breathe smoke. "I want to spare Ellen that kind of trouble!" Bon exclaimed.

"Can't spare other people trouble," said L.J. He took his Bible off the shelf above the kitchen table. "Let's go find the shovel, Ellen, and have ourselves a funeral."

The shovel was easy enough to find, standing on the porch beside the door. So was the rabbit, at the top of the can of garbage. A buzz of flies rose from its fur as Ellen raised the lid, and a putrid smell made her turn away. L.J. handed

her a clean white folded handkerchief from his back pocket. She shook it out and laid it over the rabbit's body, tucked it around, and picked the little bundle up.

"Where?" asked L.J.

"Under the zinnias."

They walked across the yard to the garden. L.J. handed Ellen the shovel. She dug a hole beside the row of zinnias, then tunneled in under a big plant with yellow flowers, trying not to disturb the roots. "It isn't easy," she said, panting.

"No," said L.J. "It isn't easy, but it's a good thing to do."

Ellen reached into the hole and down the tunnel and laid the rabbit in the cool earth. She stood up, brushing her hands, and L.J. held the Bible to his chest.

"Ashes to ashes and dust to dust," he said.

"Let this baby rabbit make the flowers grow," said Ellen. "And let him live forever in the cornfields up in Heaven."

From behind her, she heard the silky rustle of Bon's dress. "For everything there is a season under the sun," Bon said. Her words sounded biblical.

Ellen was astonished. Dad had always said that Bon could never admit she was wrong. Was she admitting something now?

"A time to live, and a time to die," said Janet. "The sun sets, but it also rises."

Ellen shoveled the pile of dirt back into the hole and patted it down firm. Janet had a paring knife in her hand. She picked a bouquet of zinnias—red, yellow, pink, orange, and white ones tinged with green. These she handed to Ellen.

One by one, Ellen laid the flowers on the rabbit's grave. She filled the bucket that stood by the pump and poured the water on the loosened earth.

Taking Janet's knife, Bon picked one more red zinnia and put it with the others. Her actions almost seemed like an apology, but that couldn't be. Bon hardly ever apologized.

Ellen turned away. Silently she and Janet, L.J. and Bon went back to the kitchen, where Queenie pranced, wondering what she had been missing beyond the screen door.

Water Under the Bridge

Bᴏɴ ᴀɴᴅ Eʟʟᴇɴ peeled the apples, while Janet rolled out pie dough on the kitchen table, and L.J. sat beside her, sipping a cup of tea. Nobody talked.

Janet let Ellen slide the pie into the hot oven. She shut the oven door with a feeling of accomplishment. "How long will it take?"

"About an hour," said Janet.

Ellen turned to Bon. "Can I go to the creek?"

"Good idea," said Bon. "Our school used to stand near the bridge." She smiled, remembering. "I loved that place, but I haven't been down there in years. I'll come with you."

"Me, too," said Janet.

"Me, too," said L.J.

They walked together down the gravel road, on the side that faced the traffic, if there had been any traffic. Queenie trotted on ahead, tail wagging high. Ellen skipped behind the dog, while L.J. made his long legs stretch farther, trying to keep up. Bon and Janet straggled behind, chatting arm in arm. Bon let her good shoes get dusty without a fuss.

At the bridge, Ellen and L.J. waited to help the others down the bank. They went down under the willows, below the bridge, slipping a little on the slope's damp grass. Ellen took off her sneakers, rolled up her jeans, and waded into the creek.

"You don't get all the fun," said L.J., pulling up his pant legs and his long underwear. His legs were skinny and white. "Let's build a dam."

"You two don't get all the fun," said Janet, kicking off her shoes and wiggling her bare toes. "When Maryann and I were in school, our classmates called me the engineer. I can build a dam." She waded in with the others.

Bon sat down on a rock, then stood, then sat again, taking in the splashing and laughter.

"Last one in's a rotten egg!" called Janet.

"Rotten or not, if you think you're going to leave me out," said Bon, "you're mistaken." She turned her back to L.J., hiked up her lavender dress, and unfastened her garters. Ellen watched, fascinated, remembering Mom's remark that Bon had refused to wear pantyhose when the fashion changed. She saw Bon roll her nylon stockings down and pull them off her feet. Then she followed the others into the water.

While they watched, Bon waded out to the middle of the stream, where the water was knee-deep. Suddenly she lost her footing on the slippery rocks. "Whooop!" She threw out her arms and one leg, trying to regain her balance, but she fell with a huge splash.

Ellen rushed to help her. Bon came up for air,

sputtering and pushing her wet hair out of her eyes. She sat on the creek bottom, with the water around her neck and her mouth wide open.

Ellen began to laugh. Bon put on her hawkish scowl. Then it fell away as laughter overtook her, too. "Laugh at me, you little squirt!" She cupped her hands and splashed Ellen right in the face.

Ellen screamed and splashed her back. Bon screamed and splashed harder. Behind them, Queenie barked and L.J. and Janet laughed as the water churned and rained down on everybody.

A rock under Ellen's foot rolled and turned her topsy-turvy. She landed in Bon's lap. Her grandmother wrapped Ellen in her arms.

"Act like a lady!" said Ellen.

"Oh, Ellen, we're so much alike, you scare me," Bon said.

Then Bon and Ellen, grandmother and granddaughter, held their noses, lay back side by side on the underwater rocks, and let the river wash them clean.